FOUR-LEGGED LEGENDS of MONTANA

Other books by Gayle C. Shirley

Montana Wildlife: A Children's Field Guide to the State's Most Remarkable Animals

M is for Montana

C is for Colorado

A is for Animals

Where Dinosaurs Still Rule (co-author)

Other books illustrated by John Potter

The Battle of the Little Bighorn

Colter's Run

Make Me a Moose! With No Fleas Please

Sis's Revenge

It's Tough to be Small in the Big Outdoors

Deer Talk

Elk Talk

The Elk Hunter

Four-Legged Legends of Montana

By Gayle C. Shirley

Illustrated by John Potter

Helena, Montana

For Sue and Chris Toppen,
special friends

Shirley, Gayle Corbett.
Four-legged legends of Montana / by Gayle C. Shirley ; illustrations by John Potter.
p. cm.
Includes bibliographical references (p.) and index.
ISBN 1-56044-222-0
1. Famous animals--Montana--Juvenile literature. [1. Famous animals. 2. Animals.] I. Title.
QL793.S48 1993
599.09786--dc20 93-29448
CIP
AC

Printed in the United States of America

Falcon Press Publishing Co., Inc.
P.O. Box 1718
Helena, Montana 59624
1-800-582-2665

Contents

ACKNOWLEDGMENTS

It's a rare book that is the product of only one person's efforts. I had the help of many obliging people while writing *Four-Legged Legends of Montana.* For sharing their knowledge, lending their moral support, and reviewing parts of my manuscript for accuracy, I'd like to thank:

Pauline Bayers, Twin Bridges, Montana; Jay Belden, Great Falls, Montana; Nancy Gale Campau, Spokane (Washington) Public Library; Bob Close, Great Falls; Terry Cloutier, Holt, Missouri; Bob Doerk, Great Falls; Phyllis Hall, Stanford, Montana; Jon Malcolm, National Bison Range, Moiese, Montana; Doug McChristian, Little Bighorn Battlefield National Monument, Crow Agency, Montana; John McMorrough, Olathe, Kansas; Steve McSweeney, Fort Benton, Montana; Kathryn Wiese Morton, Museum of Natural History, University of Kansas, Lawrence; George Ostrom, Kalispell, Montana; Jim Pyland, Missouri Department of Conservation, Kansas City; and last but most of all Dave Walter, Montana Historical Society, Helena, Montana.

". . . all other animals, at least in their natural state, can continue to exist quite comfortably without humans, but humans may be doomed without animals."

from preface to *Humans and Animals*
edited by John S. Baky

INTRODUCTION

Ever since man uttered his first words, he's considered himself supreme ruler of the natural world. But he's first and foremost an animal. He can't avoid sharing important, if ambivalent, relationships with the other species that inhabit the earth.

Generally, man tends to perceive the rest of the animal kingdom in one of four ways: as pets, prey, pests, or slaves. And sometimes the boundaries between these grow murky. Twelve thousand years ago, man befriended the dog, his faithful companion and "best friend." Yet the wolf, the dog's close cousin, has long inspired more hatred than almost any other creature. He's even the villain of many of our traditional fairy tales.

We humans can't help but be fascinated by animals. We search for and celebrate their likenesses to us but grow uneasy with their differences. Author Edith Wharton once wrote in her diary:

> I am secretly afraid of animals—of all animals except dogs, and even of some dogs. I think it is because of the us-ness in their eyes, with the underlying not-us-ness which belies it, and is so tragic a reminder of the lost age when we human beings branched off and left them: left them to eternal inarticulateness and slavery. "Why?" their eyes seem to ask us.

In *Four-Legged Legends of Montana,* you'll get a sense of this love-hate relationship man has with his fellow beings. Some of the animals featured here were cherished for their loyalty or admired for their strength or intelligence. Others were reviled because their efforts to survive interfered with our own interests.

As you read this book, you'll see that man's attitudes toward animals can change over time. Where once we did our best to exterminate the wolves and grizzlies, today we afford them special protection, to make sure they stay with us in this world. But that's not to say those deep, dark feelings don't still exist. We continue to weigh our responsibility to the creatures we walk among. Is it our job to prevent their extinction? Even if the needs of those species conflict with our own? By now we know there are no easy answers.

The animals whose stories you're about to read were selected because they stood out, even among their own kind, and captured our imaginations. All of them achieved some measure of fame not only in Montana, but nationwide. Because we thought them unique, we bestowed names upon them and kept their legends alive. Even with the passage of decades, they and their stories still stir our hearts.

SEAMAN

EXPEDITION MASCOT

"Whatever his fate, [Seaman] is part of our country's history. With fidelity and courage, he participated in an historic event which had a profound effect on our nation's future. He had been true to the pact made eons ago between man and dog."

Ernest S. Osgood
Montana, the Magazine of Western History
Summer 1976

The men of the Lewis and Clark Expedition were exhausted. All day in the rain, they had towed their dugouts and pirogues up the Missouri River, slogging through sticky, wet gumbo that sucked at their moccasins. Above them loomed the spectacular, sandstone cliffs of the Missouri Breaks in what is now central Montana. Ahead lay the intimidating Rockies, which they thought they'd glimpsed only two days earlier, on May 26, 1805.

The explorers must have been grateful to set up camp that night. After a dinner of wild game, they lay down to sleep, fidgeting until their bodies fit comfortably against the contours of the land. Captains Meriwether Lewis and William Clark at least had a tent over their heads. The others, except for the sentries, huddled under their blankets and gazed up into a rumbly, cloud-black sky.

Sometime during the night, a large, dark form slipped into the Missouri and swam toward the shore on which the explorers were camped. Clambering over one of the pirogues to reach dry land, it charged straight for the spot where the men were sleeping. It missed crushing their heads by inches.

As the men wrenched themselves awake, they must have wondered what calamity was upon them now. Was this one of those horrible grizzlies that had terrorized them for the past six weeks? Could it be an Indian attack? They scrambled to their feet, grabbing their guns. The camp was in an uproar.

The shadowy creature swerved toward the captains' tent, gaining speed. It seemed about to trample the two leaders when another black shape moved in the night. Barking furiously, Captain Lewis's dog Seaman flew at the frenzied beast—a bull bison—and forced it to change course. It galloped harmlessly into the night.

Once again, Seaman had proved his worth to the expedition. Like the other members of this stout-hearted bunch, he was loyal, brave, and strong. He was a good hunter as well as sentinel, and he proved an effective public-relations tool among the Indians. He was all any man could want in a dog—and more.

Lewis bought Seaman for twenty dollars, probably during the preparation for his voyage of discovery. The black Newfoundland was a good choice of companion. His ancestors had lived among the Basques of northeastern Spain, herding sheep and protecting them from preda-

FALCON PRESS PUBLISHING CO
PO BOX 1718
HELENA MT 59624-9948

tors. The breed also took readily to the water and was popular among Basque fishermen. Because of its water-resistant coat, webbed toes, and great size and strength, the Newfoundland could rescue men swept overboard into the icy sea. In fact, the dog was believed to have natural lifesaving instincts—a trait that Lewis would have found attractive.

For more than a hundred years, historians believed that Lewis called his dog Scannon. Then, in 1985, historian Donald Jackson made a "mildly startling" discovery. While studying the way Lewis and Clark chose names for the geographic features they encountered, Jackson was perplexed to find that Lewis had given the name Seaman's Creek (now Monture Creek) to a tributary of the Blackfoot River. He accounted for this oddity in *Among the Sleeping Giants: Occasional Pieces on Lewis and Clark*:

> No person named Seaman is known to have been associated with the lives of either captain, and as a common term the word seemed strangely out of place in Montana.... The thought occurred to me that the name might be a garbled version of Scannon's Creek, to commemorate the dog.... But when I consulted microcopies of the journals... what I learned instead was mildly startling: the stream was named Seaman's Creek because the dog's name was Seaman....

As Jackson went on to point out, ink has a way of spreading over the years, so that an *e* might fill in to resemble the letter *c* and an *m* might be misread as *nn*. To a person aware of the correct name, it fairly jumps from the journals of the expedition. Certainly Seaman is a logical name for a dog whose forebears were so linked to the sea.

Lewis first mentioned Seaman in his journal almost a full year before the expedition officially began. On August 30, 1803, after a series of frustrating delays, Lewis and a party of about eleven men finally left Pittsburgh and headed down the Ohio River to the Missouri. One hundred miles downstream, Lewis noticed a number of squirrels swimming the river. "I made my dog take as many each day as I had occasion for...." he wrote. "I thought them when fryed a pleasant food." He would discover later that Seaman was capable of landing much larger game.

At the junction of the Ohio and Mississippi rivers, Lewis and his party met a group of Shawnees and Delawares living on the west bank of the Mississippi. One of the Shawnees took a fancy to Seaman and offered Lewis three beaver pelts for him. But Lewis prized the dog for his "docility and qualifications generally" for the journey, so "of course there was no bargain."

The men of the expedition spent the winter at the junction of the Mississippi and Missouri rivers. Finally, on May 14, 1804, the party that Clark described as "46 men, 4 horses, and 1 dog" headed up the Missouri, launching one of the great adventures of all time. Four thousand miles and eighteen months of rivers and trails lay between them and the Pacific Ocean.

The trials and tribulations of the Lewis and Clark Expedition are well-known, and Seaman shared in them all. Not least of these torments was the mosquitoes, especially at the Great Falls of the Missouri. "My dog even howls with the torture he experiences from them," Lewis wrote.

Yet another affliction was the sharp spines of the prickly pear cactus. They pierced the men's moccasins, not to mention the pads of Seaman's feet. "My poor dog suffers with them excessively," Lewis said, "he is constantly biting and scratching himself as if in a rack of pain."

But Seaman did more than endure hardships. He also made his own contributions to the success of the expedition. He was a skillful hunter capable of chasing down deer and swimming to shore with antelope and beaver he drowned in the river. He could even dive underwater and drag the latter out of their lodges. Those squirrels on the Ohio had just been a warm-up!

Hunting beaver almost proved fatal to Seaman on one occasion. Lewis reported that "my dog as usual swam in to catch it; the beaver bit him through the hind leg and cut the artery; it was with great difficulty that I could stop the blood; I fear it will yet prove fatal to him."

But Seaman was made of stronger stuff than Lewis realized. Only nine days later, the dog valiantly protected his master from the sharp hooves of the stampeding bison.

Among the Indians, Seaman proved as great a curiosity as York, Clark's black servant. The big dog must have looked to them like a small, black bear with floppy ears and a wagging tail.

Three Chinook Indians along the Columbia River were so taken with Seaman that they stole him—perhaps to add to a stew. Lewis's reaction indicates how much the dog meant to him. He sent three men in pursuit of the thieves "with orders if they made the least resistance or difficulty in surrendering the dog to fire on them." For this one moment, Lewis forgot his instructions to maintain friendly relations with the Indians along his route. When the Chinooks saw the posse coming, they abandoned the dog and fled.

Seaman is last mentioned in the expedition journals on July 15, 1806, when Lewis complained about the mosquitoes at the Great Falls. Yet the party still had about 1,600 miles to cover before reaching home. Did the expedition's loyal mascot finish the journey to St. Louis? Or did his luck run out somewhere along the way? Historian Ernest S. Osgood pondered those questions and reached his own conclusions.

On July 17, Osgood noted, Lewis and three of his men separated from the rest of the party to explore the course of the Marias River. Ten days later, they took part in the only fatal skirmish with Indians of the entire voyage. The four men had encountered eight Blackfeet and camped with them along the South Fork of the Marias, now called the Two Medicine. At daybreak, the Indians tried to steal the explorers' guns, and a struggle ensued. Two warriors were killed. The rest of the Blackfeet fled, and Lewis decided it would be best if he and his party rejoined their comrades "as quick as possible." They forced their horses and themselves to near exhaustion, covering about 120 miles in twenty-four hours. Was Seaman with them? wondered Osgood.

> We know that "our dog" was an alert, vigilant and courageous guard. Would he not have raised an alarm the moment those Indians got up to steal the guns? Would he have allowed any Indian to approach his sleeping master...? If [Seaman] were with his master... it would have been impossible for him to keep up with the horses who were pushed to the limits of their endurance. Left alone on those empty plains with such predators as the wolves and grizzlies on the prowl, [Seaman's] fate would have been sealed.

Fortunately, as Osgood pointed out, there's an alternative scenario. Maybe Lewis left Seaman with the others at the Great Falls instead of taking him along to the Marias. The fact that the dog is never mentioned in the journals again doesn't prove he was killed or abandoned. In fact, it may indicate otherwise, since it seems likely Lewis would have mentioned his faithful companion's death.

Osgood believed the evidence pointed to the conclusion that Seaman was with the expedition when it arrived at St. Louis on September 23, 1806. Given the courage and loyalty with which Seaman served his master, one can't help but prefer this happier ending.

COMANCHE

SOLE SURVIVOR

"Alone from the field of slaughter,
There lay three hundred slain,
The horse, Comanche, wandered,
Keogh's blood upon his mane."

from "Miles Keogh's Horse,"
by John Hay
Atlantic Monthly
February 1879

Lieutenant James H. Bradley and the eleven scouts in his command forded the Little Bighorn River and urged their mounts to the top of the bluffs along the eastern bank. They moved cautiously, aware that Sioux and Cheyenne warriors could be lurking in the deep ravines. Only yesterday—June 26, 1876—they had seen heavy smoke and heard rumors of a catastrophic battle fought somewhere up ahead. Many of the men in General Alfred Terry's command had sneered at such nonsense. If there had been a fight, they contended, the U.S. Army would surely have triumphed. But Bradley was uneasy. "That there had been a disaster—a terrible disaster—I felt assured," he later wrote.

Bradley and his men had a panoramic view from their vantage point on the bluffs. To the west, they could see signs of Terry's troops, blue ants crawling through the Little Bighorn valley. To the south, they could see what looked like the pale carcasses of skinned buffalo scattered across a desolate hillside. They went to investigate. And so they became the first to make a grisly discovery that would shock the nation. What had looked like dead buffalo were the naked corpses of Lieutenant Colonel George Armstrong Custer and close to two hundred members of his renowned Seventh Cavalry. Some bristled with so many arrows they looked like yuccas growing amid the bunchgrass. General Terry was two days too late.

The next day, soldiers moved onto the battlefield to bury their comrades, enduring as best they could what one officer called "a scene of sickening ghastly horror." For two or three days, the remains of the men and dozens of horses had lain under the summer sun. Temperatures, according to some troopers, had climbed to more than one hundred degrees Fahrenheit in the shade—and on this hill there was no shade. By now, the stench was almost unbearable. Flies swarmed over the bloated and mutilated bodies.

As the soldiers went about their gruesome business, they discovered several mortally wounded cavalry horses and put them out of their misery. They also found one survivor of the massacre—a light bay horse riddled with arrows and bullets. Known as Comanche, he was destined to become a living legend. He would forever be remembered as the sole survivor of the Battle of the Little Bighorn.

No one knows exactly when Comanche was born, but U.S. Army records suggest it was in 1862. The brawny mustang was captured about six years later, probably in a wild horse roundup along the present-day border of Texas and Oklahoma. He was purchased by the Army for ninety dollars on April 3, 1868, and shipped along with a number of other horses to Fort Leavenworth, Kansas.

The Seventh Cavalry was stationed in Kansas in 1868, and that spring it had lost several horses in a clash with Indians. First Lieutenant Tom Custer, George Armstrong's brother, traveled to Fort Leavenworth to get replacements. He returned to his regiment with forty-one new mounts, including a sturdy, yellowish bay with a black stripe down its back, a white star on its forehead, and a black mane and tail. This horse, soon to be named Comanche, became the favorite mount of Myles Keogh, a twenty-eight-year-old Irishman and Civil War veteran. Now a captain with the Seventh, he was considered gallant by the ladies and brave but rude by many of his peers.

According to legend, Keogh named his horse on September 13, 1868, following a skirmish between troopers and a small band of Comanches. When the fighting was over, someone noticed an arrow buried in the animal's right hindquarters. As a blacksmith removed it and cleaned the wound, one soldier claimed he saw the arrow strike. When it did, he said, the horse "sure squalled as loud as any of those Comanches.... A sure enough Comanche yell." To which Keogh reportedly replied, "Comanche! That's the name for him."

Keogh and Comanche served with distinction for the next eight years, helping to quell disturbances between the Ku Klux Klan and northern carpetbaggers, escort a survey commission on the Canadian border, and ascertain the presence of gold in the Black Hills on the Sioux reservation. Then, in May 1876, they joined in the fateful campaign that would end with the Battle of the Little Bighorn.

Many Sioux and their Northern Cheyenne allies were roaming the traditional hunting grounds of what is now south-central Montana in that spring of 1876, despite orders from the U.S. government to return to their reservations. So the government decided to force them there. The plan was for General Terry's army to head west from Fort Abraham Lincoln in Dakota Territory. Meanwhile, Colonel John Gibbon would lead his troops east from Fort Ellis (where Bozeman is today), and General George Crook and his force would ride north from Fort Fetterman in Wyoming Territory. If all went well, the three forces would converge on the Indians, preventing their escape.

But all did not go well. Far more Indians were off the reservation than the Army realized, and some of them crippled Crook's column in a battle beside Rosebud Creek on June 17. The engagement caused Crook to turn back to Fort Fetterman. That left Terry and Gibbon to close in on one of the greatest concentrations of Indians ever gathered in North America—a village of about eight thousand people, a quarter of whom were probably warriors.

At the confluence of the Rosebud and the Yellowstone River, Terry decided to split his force. The Seventh, under Custer, would push up the Rosebud, cross the Wolf Mountains, and attempt to attack the Indians from the south. Keogh, on Comanche, would lead Company I of Custer's command. The rest of Terry's troops would move up the Bighorn River to its junction with the Little Bighorn, blocking the Indians' escape.

Almost everyone knows what happened next. Custer was afraid the Sioux and Cheyenne were aware of his approach and preparing to flee. So he decided to attack immediately, even though Terry had not yet arrived. Besides, he was confident his horsemen could whip any number of Indians. To the sorrow of more than two hundred families, he was wrong.

No doubt many of the troopers at the Little Bighorn faced death bravely on that fateful day. But later, the Sioux chief Red Horse recalled seeing one particular officer, dressed in buckskin, who temporarily "saved the lives of many soldiers by turning his horse and covering the retreat. The Sioux," he said, "say this officer was the bravest man they ever fought."

In his book *Keogh, Comanche and Custer*, author Edward S. Luce makes a convincing argument that this man was Keogh.

Three days after Custer's last stand, a burial party found Comanche severely wounded on the field. At first, some thought the humane thing to do was to end the suffering animal's life. But Captain Henry J. Nowlan, an intimate friend of Keogh, recognized the horse and took charge of him. One trooper later remembered the occasion:

> Many of us went over and recognized Comanche, the favorite mount of Major [sic] Keogh.... The poor fellow was too weak to stand, and many of the men mounted, galloped to the river and returned with water carried in their hats which was given the poor famished horse. Later, he was able to get to his feet and in time was brought into camp where his wounds were washed and the soreness relieved as much as possible. The story is that Dr. [Holmes] Pauling of Terry's medical staff sacrificed the larger part of a bottle of Hennesy brandy in concocting a mash for the wounded horse.

Comanche was led fifteen miles to where the steamer *Far West* lay moored at the mouth of the Little Bighorn and was taken on board along with the wounded from Major Marcus Reno's command. By the time the boat reached Fort Lincoln, the horse was too weak to stand. So he was taken by wagon to a stable and supported with a sling. A year went by before he fully recovered.

Whether Comanche was truly the only survivor of the Battle of the Little Bighorn is a matter for speculation. Author Evan S. Connell believes many Seventh Cavalry mounts survived, probably more than a hundred. Indians took the good ones for their own use. Others were unsaddled and turned loose. "One of these animals," Connell wrote, " a gray from E Company, followed Terry's column back down the valley to the *Far West;* it appeared to be terribly frightened and was last seen on the banks of the Yellowstone."

Some also claimed to have seen a dog sniffing around the hillside. And, of course, hundreds of Indians survived their encounter with Custer.

Even if Comanche wasn't the Little Bighorn's lone survivor, he was a tangible symbol of the men who perished on that summer day. As such, he was accorded special treatment. On April 10, 1878, Colonel Samuel D. Sturgis, who had lost a son at the Little Bighorn and who now was commander of the Seventh, issued General Orders No. 7 at Fort Abraham Lincoln:

> The horse known as Comanche being the only living representative of the bloody tragedy of the Little Big Horn, Montana, June 25, 1876, his kind treatment and comfort should be a matter of special pride and solicitude on the part of the 7th Cavalry, to the end that his life may be pro-

> longed to the utmost limit. Though wounded and scarred, his very silence speaks in terms more eloquent than words of the desperate struggle against overwhelming odds, of the hopeless conflict and of the heroic manner in which all went down that day.

The horse, Sturgis went on, was to be given a special stall and was not to be ridden "by any person whatsoever, under any circumstances." He was also not to be used for any kind of work. Rather, "upon all occasions of ceremony (of mounted regimental formation), Comanche, saddled, bridled, draped in mourning, and led by a mounted trooper of [Keogh's old] Troop I, will be paraded with the regiment."

For the next thirteen years, Comanche led a peaceful, pampered life, roaming the fort at will and begging for sugar lumps and buckets of beer. "The old fellow was a great pet of the soldiers," one trooper recalled. "Several times when the band would be out, or the bugles sounded for squadron formation, I have seen the old fellow trot to his place in front of the line of his master's troop."

In fact, to the Seventh he was known as "the second commanding officer" because of the unique privileges granted him.

Comanche died on November 7, 1891, at about twenty-nine years of age. The official cause of death was listed as colic. As a final tribute, officers of the Seventh Cavalry arranged to have his body preserved, mounted, and displayed at the Museum of Natural History at the University of Kansas in Lawrence. He stands there still, a monument to courage and a reminder of a way of life that is no more.

SPOKANE

CONQUERING SPIRIT

"One day, the spirit horse will return with the speed, the endurance, and the pluck of all the horses dead on the battle field. He will enter into the body of a colt, and that colt will be called Spokane, and will go forth to conquer all the horses of the earth."

Spokane Indian tradition
as told in the Virginia City, Montana,
Madisonian
June 1, 1889

The broad, arid plain reeked of blood and rang with the squeals of terrified horses. They stampeded helplessly as U.S. soldiers pumped bullets into them, slaughtering them just as the Army had slaughtered many of their Indian owners only a few days before. Finally, almost seven hundred ponies lay dead or dying. Colonel George Wright and his troops relinquished the field to the ravens.

Wright was no doubt proud of his recent victory over the allied tribes of what is now eastern Washington and northern Idaho: the Spokanes, Coeur d'Alenes, Palouses, and Pend 'Orielles. Armed with new long-range rifles, his men had routed the Indians in only four hours. But on this September day in 1858, he delivered the *coup de grace*. He knew how important horses were to the Indians. He knew they were not only a means of transportation but a sign of wealth. Without them, the Indians were powerless. And so he ordered his men to kill the captured horses, an order they reluctantly—even tearfully—obeyed.

The loss to the Spokanes, already defeated and disheartened, was irreparable. They had no choice but to accept the "peace" treaty drafted by the U.S. government. They had no choice but to give up their homeland to the encroaching whites.

It's easy to see why a people so humiliated would dream of future glory. Maybe that's what inspired the legend of the Spirit Horse. Among the Spokanes, it was said that the Great Spirit spoke to a warrior wounded in the battle against Wright. The Great Spirit promised that the souls of the murdered horses had blended into one and that one day a spirit horse—a colt named Spokane—would return to "conquer all the horses of the earth."

The Spokanes could never have envisioned the way in which the prophecy would be fulfilled.

Three decades later, in 1886, a Montana mining speculator made a visit to the wide Spokane Valley. Noah Armstrong was a shrewd and prosperous man with a finger in each of two rich pies. He was superintendent of a smelter in what is now southwestern Montana and a breeder of fine thoroughbreds at his ranch there in the Jefferson River valley.

The Spokane Valley had changed significantly in the thirty years since Wright and his troops had charged through. Trains now clattered across the vast country between the Rocky and Cascade mountains. And at the heart of this inland empire sat Spokane Falls, a booming, bustling center for agriculture, mining, and timber harvesting. More than two thousand people called the little city home.

While visiting Spokane Falls, Armstrong got word of a promising chestnut colt foaled by one of his favorite mares in his round, three-story barn back home. He decided to name the horse Spokane, in honor of the town in which Armstrong had been so graciously received.

The wobbly little animal soon began the rigorous training required of a future racehorse—at first on the indoor track in Armstrong's unique red barn. Built in tiers like a wedding cake, the stable still stands just north of Twin Bridges.

For a year, Spokane thrived on the nutritious bunchgrass and clean, dry mountain air of the Big Sky Country. His legs grew strong and his lungs powerful. In the shadow of the Tobacco Root Mountains, he raced the wind.

Then, after a year of formal training in Tennessee, Spokane tackled the real world of racing. He debuted at the Hyde Park Stakes in Washington Park, Chicago, coming in fourth in a field of five. If Armstrong was disappointed, he didn't let it stop him. He tested Spokane four more times that year. Though the copper-colored stallion won only two of the five races, he showed promise. Here was an animal to prove the worthiness of the western stables. Here was an animal worth the wager.

In 1889, Armstrong was ready to gamble for bigger stakes. He entered Spokane in the prestigious Kentucky Derby. In retrospect, it's hard to say which event that year inspired Montanans more: Spokane's performance in the "Run for the Roses," or Montana's designation in November as the forty-first state.

In the Derby, Spokane was a David pitted against Goliath. Proctor Knott, once described as "the greatest horse that ever looked through a bridle," was among the field of eight. Already, he'd won the 1888 Futurity and other important contests. Some said he was invincible. Not only that, but he was a Kentucky horse, and he bore the name of one of the state's favorite governors. He was a two-to-one favorite to win. The odds on Spokane were ten to one.

On May 9, 25,000 people gathered at Churchill Downs in Louisville to watch the fifteenth running of the 1½-mile Kentucky Derby. The day was hot and the track dusty. Women hid beneath their parasols and fluttered their palm-leaf fans. Men in high starched collars mopped sweat and dust from their brows. The betting was predictable. The people of the South backed their favorite, "betting their shirts and beaver hats on him," according to one account.

As the first few horses trotted onto the turf, the crowd responded with feeble applause. Newspaper accounts said there were titters in the stands when jockey Tom Kiley rode Spokane into view. But when Proctor Knott pranced out of the paddock, the spectators thundered their welcome. The roar startled birds and rabbits for a mile around.

With the flash of a red flag, they were off. Proctor Knott shot into a five-length lead. The gelding had won most of his races by setting a breathtaking pace early and putting an unconquerable distance between him and the rest of the field. Apparently his jockey was counting on the same tactic again. Spokane trailed in seventh place.

Not until the halfway point did Kiley make a play for the lead. Spokane sped from seventh to third, and Proctor Knott began to fade. The Montana horse, on the other hand, "still seemed as fresh and strong as a Big Sky Country wind," according to one sportswriter. The *San Francisco Examiner* reported the soul-stirring finish like this:

> Slowly but surely the fleet-footed Spokane closed in upon him like a nemesis. Only a length of daylight separated them, then a half, then as the head of the stretch was reached a mighty roar went up from the field and the grandstand. The two horses were blended in one....
>
> Then began a lull the like of which was never probably witnessed on a race track before.... There was the silence of death in the grandstand. Every eye was watching the desperate battle and breathlessly awaiting the end....
>
> On they came, stride for stride, head for head. Then, with a last mighty effort Spokane lunged ahead and passed under the wire, winner by a head....
>
> The result was almost sickening to the vast throng of spectators. Most of them would rather have seen Spokane break his neck than the record, and least of all to win the Derby from Proctor Knott.

Spokane finished the race in 2:34.5, and since the race was shortened to 1¼ miles in 1896, that record will never be broken. Spokane remains the only Montana horse ever to win the Kentucky Derby.

In the words of one chronicler, "Never on that historic spot has there ever been so great a Derby, never has that classic race been run with greater credit to the winner."

Some irate easterners argued that Spokane was just lucky. But the horse went on that year to beat Proctor Knott in the Clark Stakes in Louisville and the high-stakes American Derby in Chicago. He'd won the Triple Crown of his day, and critics had to admit that his luck lay in his swift legs and strong spirit. Who can say whether that spirit first stirred on a battlefield long ago?

Two Toes

Mighty Marauder

"Two Toes was a persistent killer. If he had slain only an occasional critter for food the cattlemen would not have cared so much. But he was a hunter who often deliberately stalked his prey and after destroying it frequently never ate a mouthful."

from *Notorious Grizzly Bears*
by W.P. Hubbard with Seale Harris

From the bluff, Kline could see the river burbling below him, a silver thread in a valley cloaked in autumn gold. It was a lovely and tranquil scene—except for the huge, yellow-brown grizzly ripping at the flesh of a horse at the river's edge. This ravenous bear, known as Two Toes, was the object of the hunter's quest.

Kline knew he had to get closer for an accurate shot, so he crept toward his prey, his rifle at the ready. As he closed in, the bear caught his scent and bolted for a small patch of timber along the riverbank. Kline fired. The bear staggered but continued its flight. Just before it reached the safety of the trees, Kline fired again. The bear bellowed as it disappeared into the heavy underbrush.

Kline could see by its bloody trail that the bear had been hit hard. Carefully, he circled the patch of trees, twice for good measure. No tracks led out of the stand. Then Kline made a near-fatal mistake. He followed the drops of blood into the timber.

The hunter moved warily, making sure he kept the giant pawprints in front of him. What he didn't know was that the bear had doubled back and was now stalking *him*. But he soon found out. With a snarl, the grizzly burst out of the brush, charging like an angry bull. Kline just had time to fire once, maybe twice, before the enraged beast was upon him. It swiped at him with its deadly claws, catching him under one arm and sending him sailing. Mercifully perhaps, Kline was knocked out cold.

When Kline regained consciousness, the grizzly was gone, but it had left its calling card: it had gnawed Kline's leg like a drumstick and broken his gun. Weak from loss of blood, Kline dragged himself to the river.

The next thing the hunter remembered was the pale blur of a prospector's face hovering above him. Kline had lain by the river all night long. Gently, the miner loaded him into a buckboard and took him to a Missoula hospital. Kline lived, but with every limping step he was reminded of his run-in with old Two Toes.

Two Toes earned his name in 1898, after escaping from a trap set by an old trapper and hunter named Ricks. While working the Mission Range in northwestern Montana, Ricks stumbled across fresh grizzly tracks. He wanted the bear's hide, so he shot and cut up a deer and set two bear traps nearby. Each one was chained to a heavy section of a fallen tree.

When Ricks returned two days later, it was obvious his bait had been discovered. The ground around one of the traps was torn up and covered with deer entrails and bloody bear tracks. But there was no bear. There was no trap. Even the log to which the trap had been chained was missing.

Following his victim's bloody trail, Ricks found the trap about a quarter of a mile downhill. The chain and log were still attached. And in the trap's relentless steel grip, Ricks found two toes and half of a bear's forepaw. The animal had chewed them off in its desperate attempt to break free.

From then on, stockmen began referring to the grizzly as Two Toes, and they soon dreaded the sight of his telltale tracks.

For the next eight years, Two Toes roamed the Mission and Flathead mountains and the country in between. To the stockmen's dismay, he soon cultivated a taste for beef and horseflesh. He seemed unconcerned about humans. At one ranch, he even climbed into a chuck wagon while the cook was away. Eventually, ranchers offered a $575 reward for his hide.

Caleb Myres, a rancher in Swan Valley, went a step farther. He contacted a hunter named Kline. But as Kline and others like him found out, Two Toes was no simple bear. After his run-in with Ricks, he avoided traps "as though there had been a sign posted beside them." He gave the same wide berth to poisoned bait. And he ripped one man's hunting dogs almost in half. Two Toes would not be easy to bring down.

On a sunny day in the fall of 1906, a man named Dale trailed a string of seven pack horses through a canyon in the Flatheads. He was ferrying supplies to his boss's outfitting camp. As the pack train reached the head of the canyon, the trail narrowed and made a sharp turn. On one side of the path was an open slope of loose rock studded with giant boulders. On the other was a dizzying drop to a turbulent mountain stream.

Two of the horses had disappeared around the bend when another of the animals gave a snort of alarm, bringing the rest to a sudden halt. Rocks began rolling onto the trail from above. Dale looked up—right into the eyes of a giant grizzly rearing onto its hind legs about twenty-five yards away.

As the bear stood, it started more rocks rolling. One hit a pack animal, which squealed and bolted in panic. And then all hell broke loose. The horses lunged against each other, trying to turn around on the narrow trail. One fell to its death in the canyon. Startled by this sudden confrontation, the grizzly charged.

By that time, the four pack horses still left on the trail were jammed together, bawling in terror. Dale's own horse pitched frantically, making it hard for him to keep the bear in sight. One moment, he saw the raging grizzly flying in his direction; the next he saw the distant canyon floor.

As Dale drew his gun, the grizzly slipped on the loose rocks and rolled over, vulnerable. Dale fired. The bear scrambled to its feet, roaring furiously, and charged again. Dale fired two more shots. Finally, the animal collapsed about twenty feet away, blood dribbling from its mouth.

It was Two Toes all right. Dale's first shot had hit the grizzly in the ribs, puncturing the lungs. The second broke his neck, and the last entered his skull above one ear. Dale dismounted, and stood "trembling like a field of wheat in a windstorm."

When Dale managed to drag Two Toes's carcass back to civilization, folks discovered just how formidable their four-legged foe had been. He weighed 1,100 pounds, about twice as much as the average grizzly, and the longest of his claws was 3¾ inches long. His body bore the scars of old bullet wounds inflicted by hunters lucky enough to get off a shot or two. The whitish hairs on his glossy coat and the condition of his teeth indicated he was about fifteen to twenty years old. He made an impressive bear rug.

Maybe Two Toes turned to raiding ranches because he found it difficult to stalk his natural prey with an injured foot. Or maybe he was simply competing for food and space on a disappearing frontier. Whatever his motive, Two Toes reportedly destroyed about $8,750 in livestock. Now his marauding days were over.

GHOST WOLF

WILY OUTLAW

"As the years pass, our wolf grows more famous. With the disappearance of his kind, he looms in grandiose style as part of the Old West, his an individual saga that will be forever sung."

Elva Wineman
Great Falls Tribune,
April 21, 1957

The Skelton brothers swung into the saddle and headed into the northern foothills of the Little Belts. Their hounds trailed them. Their rifles lay in the bed of their wagon. With grim determination, they tracked a killer.

For a week, the two men scoured the hills, lamenting the lack of snow in which to find a telltale track. They saw no trace of their quarry. Finally, disgusted, they broke camp. They loaded their belongings and began the discouraging ride home.

They hadn't gone far when something startled them and they stopped. A streak of white fur tore across the trail and vanished into the brush. They stared at each other in dismay. They had finally seen their killer—the Ghost Wolf. And their rifles were in the wagon.

By the late 1920s, when the Ghost Wolf haunted the Judith Basin in central Montana, wolves were rare. For four decades, ranchers had tried to eliminate them to protect their livestock. In 1883, they had convinced lawmakers to create the first Montana bounty. The territorial government agreed to pay a dollar for every wolf pelt presented to a probate judge or justice of the peace. As time went by, the bounty grew.

These efforts helped reduce the wolf population, but they failed to wipe it out. So in 1915, the U.S. government got into the business of predator control. It hired professional trappers to fight the wolf with poisons, traps, guns, and dogs. As a result, only about half a dozen wolves roamed the Judith Basin by 1925.

As the vast number of Montana wolves dwindled, an interesting thing happened. Ranchers began to focus their hatred on individual animals, giving them names and investing them with human characteristics. Snowdrift, the Three-Legged Scoundrel, Cripple Foot, and the Custer Wolf were some of the "renegade wolves" that terrorized the grasslands. The battle to destroy them became a personal one, and the men who killed them became local heroes.

The last of these outlaws was the Ghost Wolf.

No one knows why the lone white wolf began killing cattle. For the first few years of his life, he was a nameless hunter of deer, birds, and rabbits. But somehow, sometime, he developed a taste for beef. It wasn't long before his bloody raids became legendary.

The Ghost Wolf was first sighted in about 1915. Five years later, he was raiding cattle ranches at will, pulling down full-grown stock with apparent ease. He killed at night, often leaving his partly eaten victims alive and suffering. Later, some would estimate that he had destroyed 1,800 cattle, sheep, and horses worth $35,000. Ranchers could tolerate him no longer. They declared war on the Ghost Wolf.

Victory would not come easy. The wolf roamed a territory of more than a million acres, from the Highwood Mountains to the northern tip of the Little Belts. And he was cunning. He made wide detours around traps and poisoned bait, and he took to the mountains at the least sign of pursuit. Some said he even crouched against snowbanks to avoid being seen. In fact, the Ghost Wolf earned his name as much for his elusiveness as for his color.

One of the most dramatic incidents in the wolf's career took place in February 1930. A.V. Cheney heard a ruckus about half a mile from his ranch near Stanford. He jumped on his horse to investigate and discovered that his five Russian wolfhounds had cornered the wolf. Only one of the big dogs dared to get within biting range. It grabbed the raging animal by the tail but was so severely bitten that it finally refused to fight. Without a gun, Cheney tried to rope the wolf, but he escaped up a steep mountainside. Man and dogs chased him for three miles before giving up.

Cheney wasn't the only man outwitted by the Ghost Wolf. One rancher kept a lighted lantern hanging in his corral for two years to hold the wolf at bay. Then, one night, a high wind blew out the light. The very same night, the killer sneaked in and dined on a registered Hereford valued at several hundred dollars.

Stanford librarian Elva Wineman brought the Ghost Wolf to the attention of the nation. Her melodramatic stories of his exploits earned banner headlines in publications far and wide. Even the Associated Press picked up the news. Soon amateur and professional hunters from all over clamored to try their luck. They hunted the Ghost Wolf on snowshoes and on horseback, with dogs and with airplanes. With each escape, the wolf grew more infamous, and ranchers became more obsessed with killing him. Angry stockmen offered a $400 reward for his capture—dead or alive.

With so many people hot on his trail, the wily wolf's days were inevitably numbered. Doris Whithorn, of Emigrant, Montana, heard the story of the wolf's demise firsthand from Al Close in 1965. It happened, she later recalled, like this:

On the morning of May 8, 1930, Close was milking cows on his ranch in the Little Belts. He was interrupted by an excited neighbor, Earl Neill, who'd just spotted the white wolf nearby. Neill wanted Close to bring his dogs and help track it.

A skiff of snow dusted the ground as Close followed Mike, his little red Irish terrier, and Nick, his big black and white sheep dog, into the mountains. The dogs knew what they were doing. Close had trained them for just this occasion. They found the Ghost Wolf curled asleep in some scrub fir and charged snarling into his dreams.

The terrier clamped his teeth around the wolf's tail, while the sheep dog ran circles around them. The animals tumbled out of the brush "like an agitated sheet flapping in the wind," Close recalled. They clawed and bit their way down the hill until they were within forty yards of Close. He raised his rifle. Later, he told Whithorn:

> But I couldn't help it. First I thought of what a shame to kill such a smart fellow. Then I

> squeezed the trigger on my old Winchester and the wolf went down paralyzed. He was shot an inch below the eye. The bullet had penetrated the base of the brain. He rolled back under the low limbs of a fir tree. He couldn't move, but he was still alive. From under that tree, he snarled at me.

Close waited for Neill to catch up with him so his friend could see the wolf alive. Then he fired one more shot and broke the animal's neck. The men hung the eighty-three-pound carcass from Close's saddle for the trip back to the ranch. After showing it off there, they loaded it into the back of a pickup and drove to Stanford.

In town, word spread quickly, and people thronged the streets. Cameras clicked madly. A few special friends were allowed to pluck a bit of the snow-white fur. Men dusted off their own stories of close encounters and lucky escapes.

The Ghost Wolf's reign of terror was over. His carcass was mounted by a Great Falls taxidermist and displayed in a glass case in the county courthouse at Stanford. It stands there today, mutely snarling at passersby.

Like Close, many of the people of central Montana had mixed emotions about their legendary wolf. Yes, they cursed him for the carnage he wrought, but they felt a twinge of respect, too. Elva Wineman probably put it best:

> He was a killer, but he was a gallant animal, one to make your blood pressure mount a little higher. He gave us food for speculation for fifteen long years, as we bet on and against him. It's been awfully quiet in the Basin since he's been gone.

SNOWDRIFT

WORTHY FOE

"Those Snowdrift wolves—I simply couldn't resist their challenge. Never had they been completely outwitted. True, their big paw prints in snow or dust showed that each had lost a toe in a steel trap. But that had only heightened their prestige in the range country and given the wolfer foemen worthy of his craft."

Donald K. Stevens
Sunset Magazine
February 1925

The Ghost Wolf of the Judith Basin wasn't the only renegade wolf cursed by Montanans in the early 1900s. Several others had reputations so notorious they stand out in western history.

One of the most renowned was Snowdrift, a light gray male that worked the country between the Little Belts and the Bears Paw Mountains. During his thirteen-year career, he was credited with destroying about 1,500 head of cattle worth more than $30,000.

Snowdrift and the Ghost Wolf must have occasionally crossed paths. Both animals roamed much the same territory at about the same time. Both were large and light-colored. In fact, they were so similar that written accounts of their infamous exploits often confuse the two. Even today, the Ghost Wolf is erroneously called Snowdrift.

But in the 1920s, farmers and ranchers of the Judith Basin knew the difference. Snowdrift had lost a toe from his left foot in a trap when he was young. His distinctive track was easy to identify. He was also the first of the two wolves to meet a violent end.

After eluding scores of hunters for years, Snowdrift was trapped by Don Stevens, a government hunter, in the Highwood Mountains in May 1923. Even then the quick-witted animal refused to give up easily. He wrenched the trap free from its anchor and escaped into the timber, one front leg still clenched in steel jaws.

For four days, Stevens and Stacy Eckert, a forest ranger from the Highwoods, tracked the wolf through rough, wooded country.

"I had never known any animal to go through such country and leave so few traces," Stevens wrote later, "even with only a trap, let alone a hook-drag."

For four days, Snowdrift fled, unable to stop to hunt and eat. Finally, in a dense jungle of second growth, he could run no farther. The drag of the trap had snagged between two trees. Stevens described what happened next:

> As soon as we came near he quit struggling and sat on his tail to size us up, very coolly. Nothing coyote-like about this splendid animal, whose

> calm brown eyes held the intelligence and courage of the greatest of dogs.... We debated taking him alive for a zoo. But... we thought too much of him, perhaps, to put him in a cage....
> Eckert shot that wolf five times through the breast, two of the bullets striking the heart, as we later found, and was just handing me the gun with the last bullet in it, and telling me, with a queer expression on his face, "Put it between his eyes," when the wolf, who had been standing there snapping at each bullet as it went home, suddenly put his nose in the air and dropped dead without a sound.
> Such was the heart of Snowdrift, the outlaw.

Snowdrift reportedly kept company with another well-known wolf. The people of the Judith Basin called her Lady Snowdrift. Like her mate, she was unusually light in color and particularly fond of beef. Just weeks before bagging Snowdrift, Stevens tracked her to her den in the Highwoods and shot her between what he called "her flaming green eyes."

Two years earlier, Lady Snowdrift had given birth to a female pup that would find her own brand of fame—in Hollywood. Ranger Eckert caught and raised the silvery wolf. Known both as Trixie and Lady Silver, she starred in movies opposite the famous dog Strongheart. Snowdrift was assumed to be her father.

Snowdrift was only one of a pack of Montana wolves that became four-legged legends. Others include:

• Old Cripple Foot, "wolf queen of the Little Belt mountains." Another cattle killer, Cripple Foot earned her name by losing part of one front foot in a trap.

In 1926, Barney Brannin, a government hunter, followed her tracks to her den. When he slid off his horse to investigate, she charged out at him, snarling and baring her teeth. Unable to reach the rifle on his saddle, Brannin kicked dirt and threw stones into her face to drive her back into the den. Then he stuffed his coat and chaps into the entrance to prevent her escape. After digging a hole into the den from above, he shot Cripple Foot and her six pups, ending a ten- to twelve-year rampage that cost ranchers an estimated $20,000.

• The Three-Legged Scoundrel terrorized stockmen in the Tongue River valley for years before Percy Daily shot her near Ashland in March 1920. She had once lost a leg in a trap, but that didn't stop her from outwitting dozens of hunters.

On one occasion, a trapper dug a small cave and baited it with chicken meat, hoping to lure the Scoundrel to her death. While he waited, hidden behind a tree, the wolf slipped into the back seat of his wagon and ran off with fifteen pounds of chicken.

• Custer Wolf, perhaps the deadliest outlaw wolf in eastern Montana. After reportedly killing $25,000 worth of livestock in nine years, he was shot in 1921 by H. P. Williams, another government hunter. The animal weighed ninety-eight pounds and measured six feet from nose to tip of tail.

In a February 16, 1921, story, the *Dillon Examiner* described the Custer Wolf in words that, at least in the mindset of the times, could have applied to all these outlaw wolves of Montana:

> Many credited the story that it was not merely a wolf, but a monstrosity of nature—half wolf and half mountain lion—possessing the cruelty of

> both and the craftiness of Satan himself.... He loped through every kind of danger and passed them all. He sniffed at the subtlest poison and passed it by. The most adroitly concealed trap was as clear to him as a mirror in the sun.

Wolves seem to have been especially adept at snaring the attention and grudging admiration of Montana's human population. Why have so many of them loped into legend? Maybe Loren Daily, brother of the killer of the Three-Legged Scoundrel, had part of the answer. In 1959, he told the *Great Falls Tribune* that wolves are "one of the upper IQ varmints."

Even one government trapper, Vernon Bailey, admitted:

> Few animals are more devoted in their home life, braver or more intelligent. Yes, they were cruel killers... but even ranchmen will give them credit for their unusual intelligence among animals. Let us give them their just dues for the sterling values of affection and devotion. They are an enemy we can well admire.

SHEP

FAITHFUL FRIEND

"The one absolutely unselfish friend that man can have in this selfish world, the one that never deserts him, the one that never proves ungrateful or treacherous, is his dog."

from "Eulogy on the Dog,"
by George Graham Vest
quoted at Shep's funeral

One August day in 1936, a Great Northern train chugged into the station at Fort Benton, Montana—just as it had for countless days before. Engine bells clanged; whistles blew. Passengers jumped to the platform, and new ones clambered aboard. Railroad employees hustled to load mail bags, trunks, suitcases, crates, and milk cans.

But amid the usual bustle at the little depot that day, an unusual drama was unfolding. Part of the cargo being loaded into the baggage car was a coffin bearing the body of a Montana sheepherder. He was destined for burial in Ohio.

Only one mourner watched as the car doors slammed shut and the train pulled slowly out of the station. His tail drooped and he whined woefully. The brown and white sheep dog didn't understand where his master was going without him. He just knew he belonged at the dead man's side. With sad and puzzled eyes, he turned and trotted away.

And so began one of the most famous and heartwarming dog stories ever told—the story of a loyalty that would never die.

For the next five and a half years, the dog met every passenger train that stopped at Fort Benton—day or night, rain or shine. Always, he watched carefully as the travelers disembarked, hoping his master was among them. Always, he went away disappointed. But he never gave up.

At first, railroad employees assumed the gaunt, shaggy dog was a stray and tried to chase him away. But the dog was determined to carry out his strange mission, and everyone finally accepted the fact that he was there to stay. Sympathetic stewards on the dining cars began feeding him scraps from their tables. He wore a mile-long trail to the Missouri River where he drank, and he slept in a hollow he dug under the wooden platform.

Railroad employees decided to call the dog Shep. The name seemed appropriate. He looked and acted like a dog trained to nip at the heels of straggling sheep. Some thought he was part collie.

Ed Shields, a Great Northern conductor, was the first person to publish the story of Shep's vigil. He was the one who discovered that the dog had come to town in the company of a sick sheepherder. No one seemed to know the man's name. For three days, Shep had waited for his master outside the hospital. When the man died and his body was moved to the mortuary, Shep tagged along. Finally, he escorted the dead man's coffin to the train station. He had followed as far as he could.

Shields' story came out in 1939 in a booklet that Great Northern sold to its passengers. Almost immediately Shep became one of the most famous dogs in the world. Newspapers and magazines across the globe reported his unflagging devotion, and he was featured in Ripley's "Believe It or Not." Fan mail poured in. In fact, Shep got so many letters that Great Northern assigned a secretary to handle them.

Train travelers began asking to be routed through Fort Benton so they could see Shep. Others flocked to the prairie town by car, hoping to snap a picture. Dozens of sheepherders and others offered to adopt the dog, but station employees decided he should be allowed to live where he chose. And he obviously chose the Fort Benton depot.

Shep was a quiet, dignified dog. He wasn't interested in romping with the children who came to pet him. In fact, at first he seemed a little overwhelmed by the fuss people made. But gradually he began to accept his role as a celebrity. He grew fat and sleek on the tidbits people offered him. And he grew more trusting of the station employees who looked out for him. All that was missing from his life was the master to whom he would always be true. He was still a one-man dog.

Shep's long vigil ended on January 12, 1942. He hadn't been a young dog back in 1936. Now he'd grown old and fat. His hearing and sight were no longer keen, and he moved slower on legs grown stiff with age.

That winter morning, Fort Benton was dusted with snow. Shep stood on the tracks, watching the 10:17 train pull into the station. He'd done so many times before, always jumping to safety before the train reached him. But that day he slipped on the snowy track and fell under the wheels. He died instantly.

Perhaps Shep and his master would be reunited at last.

This might have been the end of the story if Shep hadn't inspired the affection and admiration of so many people. The news of his death went out over the Associated Press wires, right along with news of the great war that only one month earlier had devastated Pearl Harbor. Thousands mourned Shep's passing.

The people of Fort Benton planned a funeral service. On January 14, a clear, sunny day, Shep's body was placed in a wooden casket made by one of the station agents who had befriended him. Boy Scouts carried the casket from the train station to the top of a nearby hill. Hundreds joined the funeral procession—including the mayor of Fort Benton and Ed Shields, the mayor of nearby Great Falls.

A local minister delivered a eulogy praising Shep's fidelity. A bugler sounded taps, and Shep was lowered into his grave. A few weeks later, Great Northern erected a concrete and wooden monument made in the dog's likeness. It still stands guard over Shep's grave today.

Shep inspired yet another memorial. Shields decided to give profits from the sale of his booklet to the Montana School for the Deaf and Blind in Great Falls. He created the Shep Fund in 1946 with a donation of $200. He and others continued to contribute over the years, and by 1981 the fund had collected more than $50,000. Contributions continue to trickle in, although they no longer are tallied separately from other donations.

The passing years haven't dimmed interest in Shep's story. In 1960, a *Reader's Digest* article about his vigil reached an estimated twelve million readers. Other magazines have carried the tale, as have two national television networks.

Even fifty years later, Shep was not forgotten. In January 1992, Fort Benton residents held a memorial service in his honor and began raising money for a larger-than-life bronze statue of the remarkable dog. The tribute will stand in a city park beside the Missouri River.

All this fuss over a dog? *Railroad Magazine* posed the same question the year Shep died. Then it offered this response:

> Brother, you just didn't use your brain when you made that crack. Maybe you are blessed with lots of friends and relatives. We hope you are. But how many of them would show you as much loyalty as Shep gave, even unto death? Count on your fingers the number of people you know who'd be likely to meet every train for five long years in the hope of seeing you come home again.

BIG MEDICINE

SACRED OMEN

"A white buffalo was so great a rarity that even the Great Spirit must have been surprised when one was born."

Unnamed writer
quoted in "The Sacred White Buffalo,"
Natural History
September 1946

Cy Young aimed his binoculars at a white speck lying in a pasture at the National Bison Range. It seemed to be some sort of animal, maybe a mountain goat. As foreman of the western Montana preserve, Young decided he'd better get a closer look. He urged his horse forward.

As he drew near, a bison cow trotted out of the brush to protect the strange, white object. She nudged it, coaxing it to its feet. On wobbly legs, it followed her back into the brush and disappeared.

Young must have squinted in disbelief on this day in May 1933. Was he seeing a ghost? After all, only one out of five to ten million bison is born white. The odds of seeing one are "kind of like winning an $80 million lottery," according to Kim Dowling, administrative director of the National Buffalo Association.

Young must have figured no one would believe his story. He unstrapped his camera and followed the mother and calf into a ravine. After maneuvering as close as he dared, he snapped his shutter at the first white bison known to exist since the near-extinction of the great herds in the 1800s. The animal Young framed in his viewfinder would become one of the most photographed bison in the world.

With a definite lack of imagination, the staff of the bison range dubbed their new charge Whitey. The little bull wasn't a true albino. A patch of brown hair covered the top of his head like a bad toupee, and his piglike eyes were pale blue, not pink. Still, that only made him unique even among white bison. Thousands of tourists and school children flocked to see him each year.

To many of the Plains Indians, a white bison was more than a curiosity. It was special, even sacred. The Blackfeet believed such an animal instilled the power of the sun in the man who killed it. The white hide brought "big medicine," or "good medicine," to the hunter's family and band as well. Other tribes had similar beliefs. In recognition of this symbolic importance, Whitey soon became known as Big Medicine.

For twenty-six years, the white bull roamed within the safe confines of the bison range, cropping grass and chewing his cud. He grew to more than 1,900 pounds and measured six feet tall at the hump and twelve feet long from nose to tail. In his prime, he ruled the herd, siring many offspring.

When he was three, Big Medicine was bred with his own mother in an attempt to produce a true albino. The experiment worked. "Little Medicine" was born in May 1937, but the calf was blind and soon abandoned by its mother. It nursed at the udder of a Jersey cow until it was old enough to send to the National Zoological Gardens in Washington, D.C. It died there in 1949 at the age of twelve.

The average lifespan of a bison is about twenty years. By then, its teeth are often so worn it can't graze. Big Medicine died at the age of twenty-six after a life of relative leisure. During his last three years, to pamper his aging teeth, he was fed a special diet of steamed barley soaked in molasses, high-protein rabbit pellets, and the tenderest of alfalfa. Still, when he died on August 25, 1959, he weighed only about 1,200 pounds. He was deaf and nearly blind.

Since Big Medicine's death, only one white bison is known to have existed south of Canada, according to the National Buffalo Association. The animal was born in South Dakota in 1960, but it died soon after. Several white or partly white bison have been seen in Alaska over the decades. All were descendents of a herd shipped north from the National Bison Range in 1927. The Montana bison apparently carried with them the inherited albino trait.

Big Medicine's 125-pound hide was shipped to Denver to be tanned. His carcass was butchered and offered to Native Americans on the Flathead Reservation. They refused it. A white bison was too sacred to eat. The meat hung at the bison range until it spoiled. Finally, it was dumped into a gulch for the coyotes.

The Montana Historical Society commissioned Bob Scriver, a noted sculptor and taxidermist from Browning,

Montana, to make a life-sized mount of Big Medicine. According to the *Kalispell Weekly News*:

> He decided he needed the carcass to use as a model for the body mold, and on August 28 he drove to Moiese. He put a clothes pin on his nose and picked up "as much of the body as he could salvage. In spite of maggots several inches deep, we loaded the two halves in Scriver's pickup," wrote one of the men who helped him.

With the aid of several Blackfeet craftsmen, Scriver made the mold by pasting many layers of heavy paper over iron support rods—a process much like papier-mache. The finished product was a "paper sculpture" shaped exactly like Big Medicine. Then Scriver stretched the tanned hide over the mold and added artificial blue eyes he'd painted himself. The job took about a year.

In 1961, the famous animal was put on display at the Historical Society in Helena. It stands there today, occasionally attracting Native Americans who secretly burn offerings of sweetgrass beneath it. They still believe in the big medicine of this one in ten million long-shot, this symbol of the good old days when the West was wild and buffalo made their home on the range.

GIEFER GRIZZLY

TROUBLE BRUIN

"[T]here is still competition for food and space in what is known as grizzly country. But there have been few grizzlies of any note since the turn of the century. Except for the Giefer Grizzly, a go-to-hell, mean shaggy bruin in the best tradition."

Douglas Chadwick
The Reader's Digest
November 1977

One soggy day in June 1975, George Ostrom decided to check on his unoccupied cabin on Giefer Creek, just west of Glacier National Park. He had no idea he was about to play the supporting role in an inside-out version of "Goldilocks and the Three Bears."

Recent rains had washed out the bridge leading to his place, so Ostrom and his son, Shannon, stopped to borrow horses from a neighbor. Mounted, they slogged across the swollen creek. When they reached the cabin, it was obvious *someone had been sleeping in their beds*—and splintering their door, breaking their windows, overturning their stove, and ransacking their cupboards. The uninvited guest had even licked some dirty dishes clean and then stomped them to bits. Finally, to add insult to injury, the visitor had left ample, odorous evidence that he had never been potty-trained.

No, the Three Bears had not come calling, bent on revenge. All this damage was the work of one bear—a not-too-big, not-too-small, dark brown bruin that was about to find fame as the Giefer Grizzly.

No one knows for sure what tragic experiences might have turned this particular bear to a life of crime. Charles Jonkel, one of the foremost grizzly experts in the nation, thought a bigger, stronger bear may have driven it from its home territory. As a result, it may have deviated from its usual food-gathering habits.

Consciously or not, the Giefer Grizzly had managed to turn the tables on the human population of northwestern Montana. For more than a century, people had been pouring uninvited into grizzly territory, pushing the bear into smaller and smaller corners. Now the Giefer Grizzly was pushing back.

After trashing a few more cabins, the Giefer became a marked bear. So far, he'd always come calling when no one was home, but the potential for a tragic grizzly-human encounter was too great. Wildlife managers decided to trap the bear and move him somewhere he might do less harm. Because grizzlies had become a threatened species in the lower forty-eight states, the Giefer would get off easy compared to old Two Toes.

In July, wardens from the state Department of Fish, Wildlife and Parks set up a "live trap" near Ostrom's cabin. The bear simply detoured around it and raided the place again.

Next, wardens tried a cable snare, and this time they got their bear—barely. The snare only managed to nab three of the Giefer's toes, so wardens tranquilized him immediately, before he could pull loose. Unconscious and unharmed, the Giefer rode to West Glacier, where Jonkel examined him, tattooed his lip, and tagged his right ear for identification purposes. He was then taken about one hundred miles into the South Fork of the Flathead and released near the boundary of the Bob Marshall Wilderness Area. That was the last anyone saw of the Giefer—that summer.

By July 1976, the bear was back. He polished off a few more cabins in the Giefer Creek area and wound up behind bars again. This time wildlife managers strapped a radio collar around his neck, the better to keep track of his whereabouts. Then they hauled him far up the North Fork of the Flathead. Maybe he'd find this drainage more to his liking and stay put.

It didn't take long to see that he liked it just fine. He'd finally gotten the idea that the folks at Giefer Creek didn't want him around anymore. But he apparently didn't see any reason not to drop in on his *new* neighbors.

The folks of the North Fork had the pleasure of his company fifteen times before wildlife managers decided enough was enough. They let it be known the Giefer was wanted—dead or alive. The *Hungry Horse News* dubbed him "the Flathead's public enemy No. 1."

After the twenty-fifth invasion, wardens called in the "hired guns"—some full-time, professional government hunters. The bear hunt was on in earnest.

If Billy the Kid had worn a homing device around his neck, Sheriff Pat Garrett would have had an easy job of it, and a colorful folk tale would never have been born. In the case of the Giefer, his pursuers had a distinct advantage. Radio "beeps" advertised the bear's location night and day. So you'd think this would be the end of the story. But like his Old West counterpart, the Giefer was no ordinary outlaw. As one warden put it, "he's so smart one would think he had a doctor's degree."

Once, radio signals indicated that the Giefer crouched alongside a baited trap for two hours—but never did bite. When residents of the area tried to discourage his visits by placing nail-studded planks at cabin entrances, the Giefer just bent the nails as he let himself in.

By early September, the *Kalispell Weekly News* was reporting, "We are not going to actually start rooting for the bear but he certainly does deserve some respect for the way he has been outwitting the smartest hunters in bear country."

The game of hide and seek went on until the end of summer, when a puzzling thing happened. Radio transmissions indicated the bear wasn't moving anymore. Had a hunter finally caught up with him? Had he fallen victim to some natural calamity? Wardens tracked the radio signal and found the collar. It was lying in a heap of food at a plundered cabin—minus the bear. The Giefer had managed to wrench free.

Things were mighty quiet in the Flathead Valley for a while after that. A rumor circulated that some irate North Fork resident had secretly killed the bear. George Ostrom griped, "I don't know whether to sit around with the rifles loaded or relax and enjoy the scenery."

One local newspaper proclaimed the "End of Giefer." And a handful of folks who'd admired the grizzly's spunk held a wake at a local saloon.

In an article for *Sports Illustrated*, North Fork resident Douglas Chadwick recalled how tense things were that autumn:

> Everyone was carrying guns. Few of us moved unaffected after dark and we put off leaving for town until we really needed something. We were stuck here in wild country, existing on its own terms. It was like the old days. We could no more own the night than we could scatter unused food in back of the cabin, and we could no more move through willow brush in our arrogant, careless way than we could control the movements of that one bear.

In November, a bear broke into two more cabins up the North Fork. Plaster casts of the intruder's tracks matched those of the Giefer. Then winter buried the mountains in snow, and grizzlies everywhere crawled into their dens for a long, deep sleep.

As spring approached, the Flathead Valley must have been holding its collective breath. It didn't have to wait long. On May 4, 1977, a Kalispell newspaper shouted in a giant headline, "The Giefer Creek Grizzly Is Dead." And this time the press was right.

Like many a fugitive before him, the Giefer had moved up into Canada, where he'd met his end in a one-sided shootout with the "law"—in this case Ray Koontz, a grocery store owner from Pennsylvania who was legally hunting grizzlies with a Canadian outfitter. The Giefer never saw the end coming. The first shot from Koontz's .340 Magnum rifle hit the bear in the neck and dropped him in his tracks. The hunter fired twice more for insurance.

Koontz had his trophy bear mounted, its teeth bared, one massive paw poised to swipe at some unseen menace. The animal measured 8½ feet long and weighed between five hundred and eight hundred pounds. "I wanted a large grizzly," Koontz told a reporter. "Little did I know I'd get so famous a bear."

By the end of his career, the Giefer had broken into thirty to fifty-five cabins, depending on whose tally you believe. He'd led hunters in a merry chase and terrorized residents for much of two years. But perhaps most of all, he'd reminded the people of the Flathead that they aren't the only intelligent species trying to make a home in the wilderness.

EARL

VAGABOND KING

"In the fall of 1990, when I first heard about Earl... I felt like cheering. In fact, I did cheer. 'How about that Earl?' I said to just about everybody I met. I wanted to go to Kansas City and toss him a bale of Montana sweetclover, timothy and fescue...."

Don Burgess
Bugle
Summer 1991

On a pleasant day in 1990, a resident of Independence, Missouri, celebrated his birthday with a party in his backyard. This was *his* day, and he intended to observe it with all the traditional trappings: cake, presents, food, decorations, and a yard full of friends and relatives. But in addition to the invited guests, there was one gate-crasher: a bull elk that sauntered across the lawn in the midst of the merry-making. And this uninvited visitor instantly stole the limelight from the birthday boy.

In a few sparsely inhabited parts of the country, an elk rambling through the backyard might not be such an astonishing sight. But in Independence, a city of more than 112,000 people and a suburb of even-larger Kansas City, it was an eye-popper. Why, there hadn't been any native wild elk in the state for more than a hundred years!

For several months, the mysterious elk had been making surprise appearances around town—at garage sales, PTA meetings, backyard barbecues, and other unlikely events. The switchboard at the police station buzzed with calls from dumfounded residents who'd caught a glimpse of what they variously described as an elk, moose, antelope, and "the biggest deer in the world." The elk, on the other hand, seemed unperturbed.

"During the daytime, you could stand within two hundred yards of him," one conservation official said. "When he was in this one area of Independence, we had crowds of thirty or forty people—men, women, kids, dogs barking and everything else.... He didn't seem to be alarmed."

Soon, folks were fondly calling the stranger Earl, or Big Guy.

When two motorists reported hitting Earl on a four-lane highway—severely damaging one of the vehicles but doing no apparent harm to the elk—officials at the state Department of Conservation decided it was time to intervene and trap the animal. The asphalt jungle just wasn't wholesome habitat for an elk. And besides, rutting season was fast approaching. Who knew what trouble a large and frustrated bull elk might cause.

As any elk hunter knows, elk can be mighty elusive creatures. And this one had apparently found cover in a three hundred-acre island of pasture, cropland, rolling hills, and timber smack dab in the midst of the metropolis. Never having dealt with urban elk before, conservation official Jim Pyland decided to seek advice from the experts. He contacted the Rocky Mountain Elk Foundation in Missoula, Montana.

To Pyland's relief, Mike Manzo, a member of the Kansas City chapter, just happened to be an accomplished elk caller. Manzo grabbed his grunt tube and cow call and, along with co-member John McMorrough, headed out into the pouring rain on the last weekend of September. Maybe they could convince Earl to turn himself in.

But they had no such luck. Their calls merely flushed out some curious white-tailed deer.

Next, the two men resorted to aerial reconnaissance. They borrowed an airplane and circled the area where the elk had last been seen. From the air, they could see that a set of railroad tracks, thickly lined with trees, connected the two urban areas in which Earl had most often been sighted. When they searched the corridor on foot, they found Earl's hoofprints beside the tracks.

"We finally determined that just before daylight, he would move from this particular alfalfa field, down the railroad tracks, and jump an opening in the fence," McMorrough told *Wapiti*.

Armed with this information, Pyland, McMorrough, Manzo, and several others gathered near the tracks before dawn on October 6. Soon their persistence paid off. They could hear the clomping of elk hooves on the wooden railroad ties.

Aiming at a shadow darker than the surrounding night, one of the men fired a tranquilizer dart into Earl's right shoulder. The alarmed animal jumped a fence and bolted across a field.

The party waited several minutes for the tranquilizer to take effect and then spread out to look for its quarry. A police officer soon found him snoring by a creek bed, not far from a local boys' school. Dr. Robert Hertzog, a veterinarian with the group, estimated his weight at about nine hundred pounds and his age at five years. Earl's rack sported five points on each side.

"He was just such a majestic animal even laying down sound asleep," Pyland recalled later. "He was clean. He was well-fed.... He looked like he'd been living like a king."

Now, conservation officials were faced with two questions: where did the elk come from, and what should they do with him now?

The second question required an immediate answer. So officials loaded the snoozing animal into a cattle trailer and moved him to the best place they could think of: the Native Hoofed Animal Enclosure at Fleming Park, a wildlife exhibit in Jackson County, Missouri. After a brief quarantine, Earl was turned loose in a thirty-acre pasture next door to others of his kind.

The mystery of Earl's origins would be more difficult to solve. But officials did have one clue. When captured, the elk was wearing a white, plastic collar with a radio transmitter that was marked with the number 964 and the letters "GO." Obviously the animal meant something to someone somewhere.

Pyland began making phone calls. He started by contacting game managers in nearby states. When that proved fruitless, he expanded his efforts, his calls rippling outward like water disturbed by a falling stone.

Twelve states, two Indian reservations, and eight hours later, Pyland scored. He reached Gary Olson, a wildlife biologist with the Montana Department of Fish, Wildlife & Parks. Did Olson recognize the elk and collar that Pyland described?

To the astonishment of both men, he certainly did.

In February 1987, Olson had collared ten elk from a herd in the Sweetgrass Hills, an island of upthrust magma on the northern Montana prairie. He was studying the effects of hunting on elk movements, and Elk Number 964—just a spiked yearling bull at the time—had been part of that study. In April 1987, Number 964 had disappeared. Olson could no longer get a radio fix on his whereabouts.

Now, three years later, a flabbergasted Olson and Pyland pieced together Earl's story. The celebrated elk of Missouri had apparently hoofed it there from Montana—a distance of about 1,800 miles! No elk (or any other member of the deer family, for that matter) had ever migrated that far since game managers began keeping records in the 1930s. No elk in Olson's study had ambled more than thirty miles from the Sweetgrass Hills. Earl was the undisputed king of the vagabonds.

"There's probably room for him somewhere in *The Guinness Book of Records*," Olson quipped.

Olson and other wildlife experts believe Earl first wandered north from the Sweetgrass Hills into Canada, to the banks of the Milk River. He must then have followed the Milk back into Montana to its junction with the Missouri. And apparently he continued down the Missouri through the Dakotas and parts of Nebraska, Iowa, and Kansas to Independence—"a kind of Lewis and Clark Expedition in reverse," as Olson described it. How the elk avoided hunters and the allure of other elk herds along the way, no one will ever know.

"I wish there had been a video camera strapped to his back," Olson told *Wapiti*. "What a story. It's pretty phenomenal."

Even CBS, *Outdoor Life*, and the Associated Press found Earl's spectacular journey newsworthy.

What prompted Earl to take off for the bright lights of the city? Olson and other wildlife experts can only guess. Like teenagers of the human species, spike elk often develop wanderlust and strike out on their own. Their mothers, preparing to give birth again, may even chase their older offspring away so that their new calves have a better chance to survive. It seems this particular teen-elk just overreacted.

After he learned of Earl's odyssey, Montana Governor Stan Stephens agreed to let the wandering wapiti stay where he was.

"We have more than 100,000 [elk] up here," he told the Independence newspaper. "When we found out he was being well cared for and had become a local celebrity around the Kansas City area, we thought it would be a good idea to make Earl somewhat of an ambassador for Montana's wildlife."

So Earl continues to call Fleming Park home, although park officials now call him "Montana," in honor of his heritage. He thrives on prairie grasses and supplemental feedings of corn, oats, and hay. In the years since his capture, he's sired two calves and earned a reputation as the most rambunctious and intelligent member of the park's herd. Though he's settled in and given up his radical ways, Earl hasn't lost his Montana spirit.

BIBLIOGRAPHY

SEAMAN: EXPEDITION MASCOT

Brearley, Joan McDonald, ed. *Visualizations of the Standards of Purebred Dogs of the United States.* Popular Dogs Publishing Company, Philadelphia, 1972.

Clarke, Charles G. *The Men of the Lewis and Clark Expedition.* The Arthur H. Clark Company, Glendale, California, 1970.

Ferris, Robert G., ed. *Lewis and Clark: Historic Places Associated with Their Transcontinental Exploration.* United States Department of the Interior National Park Service, Washington, D.C., 1975.

Jackson, Donald. "A Dog Named Scannon—Until Recently," *Among the Sleeping Giants: Occasional Pieces on Lewis and Clark.* University of Illinois Press, Urbana and Chicago, 1987.

Osgood, Ernest S. "Our Dog Scannon: Partner in Discovery," *Montana, the Magazine of Western History.* Summer 1976.

Stoutenburg, Adrien, and Laura Nelson. *Scannon: Dog with Lewis and Clark.* Charles Scribner's Sons, 1959.

COMANCHE: SOLE SURVIVOR

Amaral, Anthony A. *Comanche: The Horse that Survived the Custer Massacre.* Westernlore Press, Los Angeles, 1961.

Bradley, Lieutenant James H. *The March of the Montana Column.* University of Oklahoma Press, Norman, 1961.

Brown, Barron. *Comanche.* Sol Lewis, New York, 1973.

Connell, Evan S. *Son of the Morning Star.* Harper & Row, 1984.

Dary, David. *Comanche.* University of Kansas, Lawrence, 1976.

Dustin, Fred. *The Custer Tragedy: Events Leading Up to and Following the Little Big Horn Campaign of 1876.* Edwards Brothers, Inc., Ann Arbor, Michigan, 1939.

Luce, Edward S. *Keogh, Comanche and Custer.* 1939.

Utley, Robert M. *Custer Battlefield: Official National Park Handbook.* Division of Publications, National Park Service, U.S. Department of the Interior.

Willert, James. *Little Bighorn Diary: Chronicle of the 1876 Indian War.* James Willert, publisher, La Mirada, California, 1977.

SPOKANE: CONQUERING SPIRIT

Bidwell, Ralph. "Spokane, Montana's Lone Derby Winner, Won by a Flaming Nostril," *Great Falls Tribune*, Great Falls, Montana. May 7, 1977.

Clark, Helen. "Montana's Winner of the Kentucky Derby," *The Western Horseman*. November 1959.

Clarke, H. McDonald. "Spokane, the West's Great Horse," *The West*. December 1964.

Durham, Nelson W. *History of the City of Spokane and Spokane County*. S. J. Clarke Co., Spokane, Washington, 1912.

Faust, Homer. "Spokane, a Montana Horse, Won Fame," *Tribune of Shelby*, Shelby, Montana. May 16, 1932.

McDonald, Claire. "Montana's Past Holds Kentucky Derby Winner," *Great Falls Tribune*, Great Falls, Montana. May 5, 1957.

Nardinger, Susan R. *Spirit Horse of the Rockies*. Spirit Horse Enterprises, Great Falls, Montana, 1988.

Pratt, Grace Roffey. "Montana's Kentucky Derby Winner," *The Western Horseman*. January 1976.

"Running of Kentucky Derby Brings Memories of Day Montana Horse Won," *Helena Independent*, Helena, Montana. May 9, 1938.

"A Spirit Horse," *The Madisonian*, Virginia City, Montana. June 1, 1889.

"Spokane, Historic Ruby Valley Horse, Won Derby on 'Spirits' of Indian Horses," *The Madisonian*, Virginia City, Montana. December 27, 1963.

TWO TOES: MIGHTY MARAUDER

Chadwick, Douglas. "The Grizzly's Rage to Live," *Sports Illustrated*. July 18, 1977.

——. "Outlaw Bear," *The Reader's Digest*. November 1977.

Hubbard, W.P., in collaboration with Seale Harris. *Notorious Grizzly Bears*. The Swallow Press, Chicago, 1960.

GHOST WOLF: WILY OUTLAW

Close, Bob. Interview with author, Great Falls, Montana. March 19, 1993.

Lindler, Bert. "Ghost Wolf Took $35,000 in Livestock," *Great Falls Tribune*, Great Falls, Montana. May 17, 1990.

Mac, 'Tana. "The Ghost Wolf," *Great Falls Tribune*, Great Falls, Montana. April 21, 1957.

——. "Stanford Area Still Remembers Its Ghost Wolf," *Great Falls Tribune*, Great Falls, Montana. April 28, 1957.

Mattson, Ursula. "The White Wolf of Stanford: Hunted Hero, Respected Outlaw." Unpublished manuscript. Montana Historical Society, Helena, Montana.

Whithorn, Doris. "He Killed a Cagey Outlaw," *True West*. March-April 1973.

Wineman, Elva. "Bullet Kills Demon White Wolf of Montana," *The Denver Post*, Denver, Colorado. June 29, 1930.

———. "White Wolf, Foe of Cattlemen, Is Dead," *Montana Wild Life.* May 1930.

———. "White Wolf of Montana is Master Strategist," *The Denver Post,* Denver, Colorado. March 16, 1930.

SNOWDRIFT: WORTHY FOE

"Death of White Killer Wolf Recalls Other Leaders of Highwood Mountain Packs," *Rocky Mountain News,* Denver, Colorado. May 29, 1930.

Dobie, J. Frank. "Snowdrift: Lonest of the Lone," *True West.* September/October 1959.

"Famous Wolf of Highwoods Dead," *Dillon Examiner,* Dillon, Montana. May 30, 1923.

Mattson, Ursula. "Search for Wolves," *Persimmon Hill.* Volume 13, Number 3.

O'Dell, Nancy. "The Last Run of the Three-Legged Scoundrel," *Great Falls Tribune,* Great Falls, Montana. October 4, 1959.

"Old Cripple Foot, Cattle Killer of the Belt Mountain Country, Is Finally Outwitted by Trapper," Montana Newspaper Association insert. April 26, 1926.

Stevens, Donald Kenneth. "The Last Stand of the Lobos," *Sunset Magazine.* January and February 1925.

Walter, Dave. "Wolves," *Montana Magazine.* January/February 1986.

SHEP: FAITHFUL FRIEND

Deming, Bob. Interview with author. Great Falls, Montana, February 15, 1993.

"Faithful Shep Has Two Memorials," *Great Falls Tribune,* Great Falls, Montana. December 1, 1963.

Joverholser, Joe. *Shep: The Story of a Dog.* The River Press, Fort Benton, Montana, 1940.

McSweeney, Steve. Interview with author. Fort Benton, Montana, February 9, 1993.

"On the Spot," *Railroad Magazine.* May 1942.

"Recent Death Recalls Shep's Lengthy Story," *The River Press,* Fort Benton, Montana. November 27, 1963.

"Shep's Faithful Vigil Commemorated," *Great Falls Tribune,* Great Falls, Montana. January 9, 1992.

Shields, Ed. *Man's Best Friend: The Story of Shep.* The River Press, Fort Benton, Montana, 1948.

Special section on Shep's death and burial, *Great Falls Tribune,* Great Falls, Montana. January 25, 1942.

"Two Magazines Carry Articles on Shep," *The River Press,* Fort Benton, Montana. March 23, 1960.

BIG MEDICINE: SACRED OMEN

"Big Medicine." Flyer produced by the Montana Historical Society, Helena, Montana.

"Big Medicine Dies at Bison Range," *Hungry Horse News*, Hungry Horse, Montana. August 28, 1959.

Dary, David A. *The Buffalo Book: The Full Saga of the American Animal.* The Swallow Press, Chicago. 1974

Dowling, Kim. Telephone interview with author. February 10, 1993.

Malcolm, Jon. Correspondence with author. March 6, 1993.

McCracken, Harold. "The Sacred White Buffalo," *Natural History.* September 1946.

Scriver, Bob. Telephone interview with author. March 6, 1993.

Walter, Dave. Interview with author, Helena, Montana. March 3, 1993.

"White Bison, Sacred Animal, Lives Unnoticed at Zoo," *The Evening Star*, Washington, D.C. November 7, 1938.

"White Buffalo: The Facts and the Legends," *Kalispell Weekly News*, Kalispell, Montana. July 5, 1978.

Wright, Geneva E. "Big Medicine: Heap Good Magic!" *Farms Illustrated.* September 1946.

GIEFER GRIZZLY: TROUBLE BRUIN

Chadwick, Douglas. "The Grizzly's Rage to Live," *Sports Illustrated.* July 18, 1977.

——. "Outlaw Bear," *The Reader's Digest.* November 1977.

"Giefer Grizzly Continues to Elude Hunters," *Hungry Horse News,* Hungry Horse, Montana. September 23, 1976.

"Giefer Grizzly Eludes Captors," *Hungry Horse News,* Hungry Horse, Montana. September 2, 1976.

"Giefer Grizzly Killed in Canada," *Hungry Horse News,* Hungry Horse, Montana. May 5, 1977.

"Giefer Rates Readers Digest," *Hungry Horse News,* Hungry Horse, Montana. November 10, 1977.

"Marauding Bruin in North Fork," *Hungry Horse News,* Hungry Horse, Montana. August 12, 1976.

Ostrom, G. George. "About Charlie Russell, Dempsey, Grizzly Bears, Thieves, and Other Things," *Kalispell's Weekly News,* Kalispell, Montana. July 1, 1975.

——. "The Giefer Creek Grizzly Is Dead," *Kalispell Weekly News,* Kalispell, Montana. May 4, 1977.

——. "The Giefer Creek Grizzly: The Bear That Couldn't Cope," *Kalispell's Weekly News,* Kalispell, Montana. August 6, 1975.

——. "A Wrong for a Wrong," *Kalispell Weekly News,* Kalispell, Montana. October 6, 1976.

——. "Giefer Creek Grizzly Returns," *Kalispell Weekly News,* Kalispell, Montana. August 4, 1976.

"Reynolds Adds to Bear Experiences," *Hungry Horse News,* Hungry Horse, Montana. September 9, 1976.

"Weekly Griz Report," *Kalispell Weekly News,* Kalispell, Montana. September 8, 1976.

EARL: VAGABOND KING

Burgess, Don. "Pioneers on the Prairie: Wanderlust," *Bugle.* Summer 1991.

Campbell, Matt. "Big Guy the Elk is Captured," *The Kansas City Star,* Kansas City, Missouri. October 7, 1990.

Carroll, Diane. "Captured Elk Traveled from Montana," *The Kansas City Star,* Kansas City, Missouri. October 11, 1990.

"Earl the Elk Named Ambassador to Missouri," *Conservation Currents,* newsletter of the Missouri Conservation Department. November 1990.

"Elk Named Montana Ambassador," *The Examiner,* Independence, Missouri. October 12, 1990.

Etling, Kathy. "Missouri: The Kansas City Elk," *Outdoor Life.* October 1990.

"KC-RMEF Committee Members Help in Capture of Independence Elk," *Grasslands Elk News,* newsletter of the Kansas City chapter of the Rocky Mountain Elk Foundation. October 1990.

Klaphake, Penny. "Goin' to Kansas City, Kansas City, Here I Come," *Wapiti,* newsletter of the Rocky Mountain Elk Foundation. November 1990.

Olson, Gary. "Kansas City, Here I Come!" *Montana Magazine.* June 1991.

Peterson, Jeff. Telephone interview with author. May 27, 1993.

Pyland, Jim. Telephone interview with author. June 4, 1993.

Wilson, Betty. "Montana the Elk Is Alive and Well," *Lee's Summit Journal,* Lee's Summit, Missouri. October 11, 1991.

INDEX

About the Author

Gayle C. Shirley grew up mostly in Colorado and Idaho, but has lived all of her adult life in Montana. She is a graduate of the University of Montana School of Journalism. She worked as a reporter and editor at two daily newspapers in Montana before taking a job as the children's book editor at Falcon Press. Gayle lives with her husband, Steve, and sons Colin and Jesse in Great Falls, Montana. This is her fifth book.

About the Illustrator

John Potter, a Chippewa Indian artist from Lac du Flambeau, Wisconsin, has lived in Montana for eleven years. He was awarded a bachelor's degree in illustration from Utah State University and currently works as an editorial artist for the *Billings Gazette* in Billings, Montana.